Into the Night Sky
Book Five

Tricia Martin

The Old Tree Series

Request for information
Contact Tricia Martin at
t.martin@dslextreme.com

To Michael Martin
Because of your love for reading,
especially fantasy adventures,
this series is dedicated to you.
Someday you will give these stories
to your own children to read,
and that will make me laugh
with joy.

Contents

Into the Night Sky
Book Five

Tricia Martin

Chapter One

The Chariot

Sitnaw turned the hat over in his hands and shook his head. "Get rid of this ridiculous thing."

Three darkly hooded arcs bowed and took the strange hat from their leader.

"Find a place to hide it where the Bizians will never find it." A cruel smile slowly covered Sitnaw's face.

"Yes, your Majesty." They said in unison as they bowed and slowly moved backward toward the door.

****

Philip sat on his bed with the diary laid out in front of him. His grandmother had given it to him, hoping he'd express his feelings in writing. This was going to be his very first entry so he wanted to take his time.

Deep in thought he picked up the pen, sat for a moment and then began to scribble in the journal. It went something like this:

Dear reader: I'll begin by

telling you about a boy I met today as I was walking home from school. I noticed him earlier in one of my classes.

"Hey Phil, wait up!" he called out to me. His name is Mike and he has a short mop of blond hair and a big smile.

And reader, he appears intelligent, which is important to me as I do not waste my time on those who are silly and frivolous, but I prefer deep thinkers and those interested in life's mysteries.

I introduced myself. "Hi, Michael, and please called me by my full name Philip. How are you?"

"Do you really want me to call you Philip? Well, please call me Mike, not Michael. What're you doing today?"

"Studying and reading," I said.

Reader: I enjoy spending time after school learning new information from my various books. Sometimes I set up interesting scientific experiments. Those my age don't understand my activities and make fun of me. But I noticed immediately that Mike was different.

He said to me. "Hey, what about coming over for a swim?"

Hmmm, I had to think about that for a minute. I am shy with pale freckly skin and just arrived here from England at the beginning of the school year.

I never participated in sports in England with the weather and all. It suited me just fine to sit in the house and read, write and study.

School is almost out for the summer and Junior High has been boring, I really don't like it.

Well, today I felt like I needed to expand my horizons and meet some new peers my own age, so I thought over Mike's invitation and accepted it

I found out that I live one street over from him so we made a quick stop at my house to get a bathing suit.

Mike's home was on the corner and quite nice. He had a huge backyard, almost twice the size of mine, with a pool. I slowly lowered myself into the water after Mike got me wet by jumping in and creating a huge splash. I located a raft and spent the rest of the day floating around on it.

Mike's mother brought out pretzels (his favorite), lemonade and licorice, which was tasty. I did *save a few pieces for Mike.*

We got on well, Mike and I. He is smart too and able to spar with me on many difficult topics. I spent the rest of the day floating in his pool and then headed home to rest. It had been a long physically strenuous day for me.

Well, I am now at the end of an exhausting day even though I enjoyed swimming with my new friend, Mike. But it is nice to be back home and up in my room resting.

My grandmother has already gone to bed. Old people need a great deal of sleep. But I asked her permission to stay up and read for a while. I don't think she expected me to stay up quite this late, but I am reading a story about two children who go on wonderful and exciting adventures with a prince.

Whoa! What was that thump out front? Reader, I just went and peeked out the blinds of my bedroom window. I know Christmas is not in the summer so what I am looking at is obviously not Santa and his sleigh. This does not make sense. In front of my house is a chariot with two horses standing on my front lawn.

Do you know what I mean by a chariot, reader? It is a two wheeled horse-drawn scooter or car. You stand up in it. Hey, I looked that up in my dictionary. I like looking words up. The chariot is a deep royal blue with flames of white, yellow and orange on the sides, giving it the appearance of being on fire.

I have already rubbed my eyes

several times and decided - as my parents taught me - that if some-thing does not make sense to the mind then it is illogical.

Closing my eyes and then opening them again, the chariot remains, looking as if it is waiting for something. Out of the corner of my eye a minute ago, I saw a commotion and now a boy and a girl are standing beside the chariot, talking in hushed tones.

Reader, this sort of thing is very stimulating to my brain. I like to investigate new and strange things and this is certainly new and strange, very strange.

This is probably a dream. I know if my mother was alive, she would have a good explanation for what is going on.

Well, I'm now going outside,

to investigate the boy, the girl and the chariot, in the middle of the night. So goodbye reader.

This could be my last entry.

****

Philip closed his journal, put his pen down, got off his bed, and slowly turned toward the door of his bedroom.

Chapter Two

A New Adventure

Mike and Mari took in their surroundings. This must be another adventure Bob had whisked them into. It was late at night and street lamps shined down on the front lawn of a house similar to theirs.

Mike recognized the street as

the one his new friend, Philip, lived on. But whose house were they standing in front of, now? Could it be his new friend's house? Looking up, Mike saw the shape of a boy in the upstairs window, peaking out at them through the blinds.

"Hmm, this has to be Bob's doing." Mari peered up at the shape silhouetted against the window.

"It's obviously Bob, but it doesn't seem like the adventures we've had in the past." Mike turned to face Mari but could barely make her out in the darkness.

Both of them had been on several adventures with their friend, Bob. Each one started in a park near their homes where they had discovered an unusual tree; the colors were more vibrant, with deeper greens and richer, stronger browns than in other trees they had seen. At the beginning of each adventure the trunk would open up, creating a gap large enough for them to crawl inside.

The interior floor of the tree was covered with grass and tiny, delicate flowers of every color planted around the edge. The walls were smooth and dry and softly lit by a source that filtered down from above.

In the first adventure a small dog named Spot had welcomed them and invited them to tea. Then they met Bob and while traveling with him, found out he was a great Prince and ruled a beautiful Kingdom. Through several adventures, Bob and the children helped people of various worlds.

"Well, one thing's sure; this is the same chariot we used when we searched for that lost book." Mike looked over at Mari in the dark. He had now traveled under the water, into space and to several strange lands.

"Oh yeah, it does look like it, but where's Bob." Mari looked puzzled. "It's weird that he isn't here and we're standing by this chariot instead of the old tree. Very strange."

They both looked up and studied the shadowy shape in the second story window.

Suddenly, standing right in front of them, was a round, short person with hair that went up to a point on the top of his head. He was wearing bright blue overalls and had a shape similar to a small bear cub. A second round, short person appeared right next to him with bright red overalls.

"Mike and Mari, how wonderful to see you again," the first little person said.

"Aire!" Both yelled in unison.

"It's so good to see you." Mari threw her arms around him and gave him a big hug. She turned to the other little person. "Hello, I'm Mari. What's your name?"

Aire turned toward his little friend. "Oh! Please excuse my manners. Mike and Mari, this is Nob. He's my assistant and I am training him in the art of governing Bizia."

Nob smiled and extended his hand to shake Mari's.

"How are things in the land of Bizia?" Mike focused on Aire.

"Since you left, our land has been peaceful, and has returned to the ways of the past. The people are happy and contented again. Thank you, both of you."

Bob had taken Mike and Mari to the land of Bizia. While there, they discovered that the Bizians were fun-loving and playful, and liked to sing, dance and perform poems and stories for one another. But something had gone terribly wrong, causing an imbalance in their land. Bob, with the help of Aire, Mike and Mari, restored it to what it once was.

Mike focused back on the house and suddenly the front door opened and Philip, his new friend from England, stood in the door frame with the porch light shining down on him.

He walked toward the small group. "Michael, what is going on here?"

"Hey, Phil, I-I mean Philip — you really want me to call you Philip? Remember, call me Mike. Anyway, we were just about to ask you the same thing."

Philip examined Mike and the other three people standing on his front lawn. He stood for several minutes inspecting Aire and the other Bizian, Nob. Then he went over to the chariot and stared at the two horses pawing their feet and snorting.

Pulling out what looked like a small journal, he begin writing in it while he talked to himself.

"Is he okay?" Mari pointed at Philip. "That was a strange reaction to seeing Aire and Nob."

"Oh yeah, I hung out with him today. He's from England. A little different. Likes to study and loves science fiction. This is probably right up his alley. He enjoys reading stories about space and told me there was a possibility of life on other planets. Aire would intrigue him."

"No, I mean is he going to be okay? He's talking to himself."

"I am writing in my diary." Philip turned and looked straight at Mari. "My mum taught me to write down every possibilities in any situation that did not make logical sense. So, that is what I am doing. Also, my parents told me to ask questions and get to the bottom of any situation quickly. Oh, and by the way, do not call me Phil. Call me Philip, please."

"Well, I'm Mari, by the way." She felt uncomfortable and self-conscious, realizing he had heard her comment.

"Hello." Philip looked past Mari. "And who are these little creatures? Very strange indeed. Now I'm sure this is a dream." Philip pointed to Aire and Nob and he was ready for answers.

Mike stepped toward him. "Philip, this is Aire and his assistant Nob. They're from the land of Bizia. Aire's the Governor of that land. A wonderful place that Mari and I visited. We went through a tree - Oh boy. Never mind. It's a long story.

"No, go on please. This is interesting." Philip continued to write in his journal. At that moment they were interrupted by the two horses pawing their hoofs on the ground and snorting loudly.

"These guys look like they're ready to go someplace and fast." Mike walked closer to the chariot. The small group joined him.

"Wait, please. Don't get on the chariot until I explain." Aire stood in front of the doorway with his arms stretched out to block Mike and the others from climbing in. Nob stood at his side ready to assist.

Now remember Bizians love to tell stories, so of course Aire began. "Now, let me tell you three why we're all here, in the middle of the night, looking at a chariot, in Philip's front lawn."

Aire moved into the chariot and stood facing them with Nob at his side. "When Sitnaw, the evil one, finally left our world, he took something valuable with him. We failed to notice it missing at first."

He sat down. "When our land was established, Prince Bob and his Father placed a kind, strong leader in our midst; to govern us and help keep the guidelines we had been given. Our people made a special hat for that leader to wear, and it has been handed down from Governor to Governor throughout the years."

Mike noticed Nob's head bob up and down in response to the storytelling. He seemed engrossed in what Aire was saying.

"Then, Sitnaw, an evil arc, came to rule our land, causing chaos and confusion. We didn't realize that when he left he took the Governor's Hat and the authority it represented with him. Even though everything's been restored to its original state, thanks to you, and of course Prince Bob, we don't have the Governor's Hat. Sitnaw has it."

"What does it look like?" Mike asked.

"Like a top hat with blue and green stripes vertically on its sides and the top is red. It's fun to wear and represents the creativity of the Bizian people as well. The Hat is a symbol of the order and authority in our land and the Governor wears it with pride."

Aire was about to continue when Philip walked up to him, and interrupted his story by blurting out, "and why are we involved in this adventure, and the chariot, why is that here? Oh! And who are you again? And what am *I* doing here, when I have nothing to do with Bizia?"

Mike remembered Philip's comment that his parents had taught him to ask questions and get to the bottom of any situation quickly. He was certainly doing that, and rather rudely.

Aire, being the gracious and kind Bizian that he was, smiled at Philip. "Good questions, Philip. Mike and Mari helped Bob restore our land and rid us of Sitnaw and his followers. We thought they might want to help find the Hat as well. As to the chariot being here, that's our means of transportation. You see, Sitnaw and his minions are equipped to travel into space and we believe they've taken the Hat there. This chariot is also able to journey into space. Well, I've finished my story now, you can all move inside the chariot and we'll begin the adventure."

Chapter Three

The Chariot Ride

As Aire waved them onto the chariot, Mike looked over at Mari and she saw the excitement in his eyes. The anticipation of a new adventure filled her with delight and she suddenly felt like she could fly. Another adventure was waiting for her and she was ready.

Philip stepped up to Aire. "How do I know that this quest for the hat is for me? I can understand Mike and Mari being involved, but I don't know anything about Bizia." Philip had brought up a good point.

Mari wondered why he was part of this adventure as well. It was strange that the chariot wasn't near the old tree, or in front of her or Mike's home, but here in front of Philip's house. Everyone turned toward Aire, eager to hear his reply.

"Have you not been searching for something since your parents died?" Aire looked at Philip with kindness in his eyes.

Everything became still and quiet. Philip turned away from everyone as he fought back tears. When he thought about his parents, it caused him such pain but he never knew what to do with the sorrow. His grandma tried to help him talk it out, but it was too raw.

"Don't worry, Philip. The Prince sent me to invite you to join us." Aire put a hand on Philip's shoulder.

"Well, if Prince Bob invited you then you were meant to come," Mike said encouragingly.

"Oh yes," Mari burst out, "You'll like Bob. He's very kind but also very powerful. Did you know he's the Prince of a beautiful realm with his Father?"

Mari noticed the high level of emotion in her voice as she spoke about Bob. She also saw Philip square his shoulders (he had been slumping) and take a deep breath.

"Well I am not interested in the emotional part of this, but the adventure sounds exciting to me. I have need of more information, therefore I have decided to join you." Philip also thought, but would not voice this, *and I'd very much like to meet this Prince Bob.*

Mari suddenly felt tired. She climbed into the chariot and sat on the bench seat that ran the length of the back.

"I don't feel good," she whined.

"Have you had anything to eat recently?" Aire looked at her with concern.

"No! I was awakened in the middle of the night and brought here."

"Wait a minute." Mike began to rummage around. "Let's see

what this chariot has in the way of food."

Nob joined him in the search and was successful. "Look." He held up a little bundle and began to pull out food and drink.

Mari perked up when she saw the supplies. Her stomach was growling and it seemed like days since she had eaten (actually the last time had been just five hours ago). *Just like Bob to take care of us. Thanks.*

Yawning, she looked though the bag and finding a pear, settled down to chew on it. *Wow, there are some interesting drinks in here,* Mari thought as she looked inside the sack. She pulled out an oddly shaped bottle of what looked like cranberry juice and began to drink it. Immediately feeling better, she sat up. *Wow, what was in that drink?*

Aire was the last one into the chariot and closing his eyes, he sat quietly for a moment. Suddenly the horses took off in a blaze. Mari saw what looked like flames of fire from the horses, being blown back toward the chariot as they climbed at breakneck speed into the night sky.

Philip sat next to her and reached into his jacket pocket pulling out the diary his grandmother had given him. As he began to scribble, Mari read over his shoulder:

Reader, I am still alive but you are not going to believe this. We just got into the chariot with a creature from another planet that looks like a small bear cub, his name is Aire, and he brought a friend with him. So there are two of these strange people from a land they call Bizia on our chariot and Aire is actually flying it.

We are moving into the night sky and beginning to leave the earth's atmosphere. The stars and planets are becoming more visible each minute. I know this sounds impossible to a rational mind, especially one like mine, but we are moving into space.

Nebulas, stars and planets surround me. I have studied astronomy so I know quite a bit about space, but this is amazing and the adventure of a lifetime. I have always wanted to be an astronaut and travel into outer space. These planets are really close and the chariot is flying right by them. It almost looks like I could reach out and touch one of them. Amazing.

At that moment Mari was distracted from Philip's diary by something ahead of them. In the distance, an enormous door had appeared in space and was slowly opening, flooding them with a bright light. It was shaped like a gigantic doorway in the heavens and the chariot headed straight for it.

As they drew closer, Mari gaped in awe. "Look at that," was all she could get out.

Philip turned toward her. "This opening is the size of many galaxies. Look it's opening more – Fascinating."

At this point they were all speechless. Blinded by the intense light, Mari could feel the presence of countless beings inside the door.

Aire moved into the entrance and hovered there for several minutes and then the chariot sped out of the opening at breakneck speed.

When Mari looked behind her, the blinding light was following them down toward earth like a comet. She suddenly realized that within the light were creatures or beings that were creating the brightness.

"Look." Mari pointed behind her at the extended streak of white light following them.

"Oh, yes," said Aire. "Those are arcs from Bob's realm. We came to gather them."

Mari turned and looked behind her again. She could see the

arcs clearly now, and wondered if Mie, her friend who had helped in the last adventure, was with them.

"Oh, I love arcs. So that's why they're following us?" Mari looked at Aire.

"We need their protection where we're going." Aire answered from the front of the chariot.

"And where pray tell is that?" Philip had now joined the conversation.

"Prince Bob told me to bring the arcs back through the old tree into Bizia."

"I don't see what the big deal is with this hat? Disturbing all those creatures or arcs or whatever you call them." Philip stood up and frowned.

Nob spoke up for the first time. "In Bizia, Philip, it's important to show respect for those placed in authority over us. The Hat is one way of doing just that."

"But the hat sounds absurd." Philip pictured it on someone like Aire and laughed. Then he coughed to cover the laugh. "I have very different ideas about authority. Now being a scientist or someone in the public eye..."

At that moment Philip was cut off as the chariot jerked and veered to the right. He decided to sit back down, but he wasn't holding on to anything and lost his balance. Reaching out with his hands to grab on to something, he realized it was too late and he fell over the side of the chariot.

As he was falling through space, he watched the flaming horses galloping down toward the planet below, a round ball with blue and green swirls on it. Philip could see the brilliant white glow of the arcs streaking down behind the chariot.

He continued to fall into the darkness below, the empty blackness of space closed around him and he could not breathe. *Well, guess this is it. They didn't even turn back to find me,* he thought sadly. Suddenly it felt like huge hands had caught him and he was being slowly lowered toward a small moon below.

He landed softly on his feet. *What was that? Guess there's some kind of atmospheric cushion around this moon.* But what he thought, tucked deep down inside, was that two huge hands had caught him, saving him from the fall.

Philip looked around, trying to take in his surroundings, but he was unable to see anything except darkness. And it was very dark. His parents had taught him to calm down and think at times like this. Mind over emotions was always the best course of action.

He leaned over to grab a fistful of planetary dust and the cold bit at his fingertips. He bent down to investigate further and when he touched the ground, it reminded him of ice cubes in his freezer. Finally he sank down onto the ground and began to cry.

Do not think badly of Philip for crying; remember he was in space, by himself, on a barren moon in the darkness. He cried and continued to cry until he realized he would need the water in his body to survive, which made him stop. A quiet stillness came over him and he felt better.

He had not cried when his parents died, even though the pain cut deep and he thought about how sad his life had been. No one was on this barren moon to hear him so he spoke out loud.

"Why has my life been so hard? What did I ever do to deserve this? Why did both of my parents have to die when I see all these other kids, like Mike, with mothers and fathers? And why don't I fit in at school? Well, actually I do have friends there, but the popular ones don't include me."

He was really getting into it now and began expressing his opinions freely.

"I think their stupid, with the

way they spend their time. I would rather read, study astronomy and do science experiments. I thought I would become famous and highly respected worldwide for my all discoveries in science. Yeah, right."

He threw the handful of dirt he had grabbed onto the ground. "Like that will ever happen now that I'm stuck on this dead moon, in outer space. This planet fits my life, alone, cold and barren."

Suddenly Philip felt the presence of someone standing in front of him in the darkness.

"W-whose t-there?" He asked in a shaky voice.

"I am here." The deep voice sounded warm, strong and kind, but fun and joyful all rolled into one.

"What are you?"

"I am that I am."

"You're frightening me. Please don't hurt me."

"Philip, I would never hurt you. I am here to help you, my son."

"Are you -?" Here Philip stopped, got goose bumps all over his body and then continued, "Are you my f-father's g-ghost?"

"No." The answer was spoken by a quiet voice filled with warmth and peace. "You have been looking for a way to be valuable, and find love. Being famous will not fill this empty place in your heart. These needs are filled from the inside out. You will never find what you seek, Philip, from becoming famous. Being a scientist or astronomer is a noble endeavor, but you have the wrong motive for doing this. Now, tell me your troubles, son, and I will listen."

Philip sat for a moment in thought. He was stuck on this rock, in space, who knows where. This had to be a dream. So for the first time since his parents had died Philip decided to share his heart with someone.

"I moved here from England with my grandmother, so I dress and look different. It has been somewhat difficult for me, as kids at school think my clothes are strange and a few of them have laughed at me."

"Go on," said the voice.

"You really want to hear all of this?"

"Yes, Philip," came out of the darkness.

Philip let out a sigh. "I lived in

England for ten years with my mother and father as an only child. They spoiled me with all kinds of sweets and interesting toys that made me use my brain cells to figure them out."

He paused for a moment.

"I'm still listening," the voice said.

Philip continued, "my mother was a psychologist, which means she helped people with their problems. My father was a corporate lawyer, which means he assisted companies with their problems: In conclusion, both my parents helped people with their problems. And then there was me, the apple of their eye and their favorite person in the entire world. I was the center of everything in my family and felt loved and special."

He stopped for a moment.

"Everything's going to be all right, Philip. Go on."

"My parents would tell me continually that I was going to be someone of great importance in our world. Then they would mention people like Einstein and Steven Hawking, explaining that they were great scientists. I spent long hours thinking about how famous I would become and the influence I would have on our planet."

Philip stopped and sighed again. With a shaky voice he continued. "Something terrible happened, and I don't like to talk about this." He paused and could feel tears running down his cheeks. "Both my parents were on a train going into the countryside, to have a few days alone together. Well, something happened to the train. It derailed and smashed into one of the stations. Everyone on the train was killed instantly. My parents were killed! They both died and I was left all alone. I can't continue-"

The voice spoke again. "It's all right. I'm here to listen. I am so sorry this happened to you, son."

Philip sniffled and wiped his eyes. "Anyway, I wasn't really left alone; my grandmother was with me when I found out about my parents. She took me in her arms and held me for a long time. Then she told me she wanted to move to America, actually California. And I thought, why not!"

He breathed in deeply and let out a long, slow sigh. "That's how I found myself, British through and through, in the United States of America, football instead of cricket, sunshine instead of rainy days and coffee instead of tea." He could feel the aching pain welling up from deep inside. And he began to cry softly again.

"You don't need to carry the pain; I will help you with it and show you how to be free." The voice sounded soft and tender.

Philip wiped his eyes with the back of his hand. "I know you've listened to everything I shared. But how can you understand when you're not a boy and have never be rejected or lost anyone to death."

The voice seemed to draw closer to Philip. "I too have known sadness and pain, my son. And I have known the sorrows of death. Others do not need to experience exactly the same situation as you to know these feelings and feel compassion."

Philip peered into the darkness. "Are y-you human? A m-m-man?" He stuttered.

Philip heard a rustling noise and suddenly, standing in front of him was indeed a man with light pouring out of him. As he gazed at the man, a deep peace and joy flowed into Philip.

"Do you want to know more about me and my Kingdom?"

Philip felt speechless and all he could get out was one word. "Yes." He dropped down onto one knee and bowed before the man.

Bob reached out his hand and pulled Philip up. Yes, it was Bob who had rescued him and lowered him down to the moon, and it was

Bob who had listened to him share his sorrow and pain.

"Will you come with me into a new life and a new way of looking at life? No longer focusing on your pain or how famous you'll be one day, but focusing on life now and finding peace and contentment in the present."

Philip did not feel the need to speak and choked out another "Yes." New feelings were flowing within him, and he knew a new life was beginning.

Chapter Four

Through The Tree

When Mari awoke, it took a few minutes to remember why she was not in her warm bed. As stars and planets raced past, she realized she was in a chariot, in space, moving at breakneck speed toward earth. How could sleep have overtaken her in this situation? *I must have been really tired*.

The chariot shot through the clouds and touched down next to the old tree in the park.

"Oh, no!" Mari cried out, looking around. "Where's Philip?"

"I don't know. Somehow I feel asleep at the wheel and just woke up as we were landing by the old tree." Aire put his furry little arm around her.

"Strange, I woke up right before we landed too. Where is Philip?" Mike stepped out of the chariot and spun in a circle looking for his new friend.

Mari slowly climbed out of the chariot, with her head hung down. As she headed for the old tree, she looked up, and there standing in front of it was Bob. He held his arms out as she and Mike ran up and gave him a big hug. Mari looked up into his face with tears in her eyes. "We lost Philip somehow. I don't know—" Her voice broke and tears fell onto her cheeks. "I think he fell out," she said softly as she let out a sigh.

Bob put his arm around her. "Don't worry, Mari, I know for a fact that Philip is fine and having the adventure of his life." He gestured toward the old tree. "I'm sending you two, with Aire, Nob and a few arcs from my Kingdom, into the land of Bizia."

Right then, Mari heard a commotion behind her and when she turned around, hundreds of arcs were landing all over the park, filling it with white light.

Bob moved rapidly through the old tree, as if it was made of smoke. Mari quickly followed Mike, dropping onto her knees with Aire and Nob right behind her. Carefully she crawled through the opening in the trunk.

When she stood up inside, she breathed in the wonderful scent of flowers and grass. Bob was standing right next to her and she felt peace flowing from him.

He waited until everyone was inside and then said, "I need to leave you but I'll be back. Take good care of them, Aire. Don't worry, Mari, everything will be all right, and Philip will make the right choice." Then he vanished.

Mari's faced dropped, "I hate it when he does that and love it when he's with us."

"I know, I feel the same way." Mike smiled at her and then looked puzzled. "Wonder what Bob meant about Philip making the right choice?"

Mari shrugged. "I'm just glad he's okay. I wish Bob had stayed." She sighed again.

Aire patted Mari's hand. "Now, don't worry. Remember our last adventure together and how it turned out. Bob will return when he's needed. Are you two ready?"

Mari and Mike both nodded. Aire walked through the door on the other side of the old tree's interior with Nob right behind him.

Mike followed and shouted back to Mari. "Hey, we're back in Bizia."

Mari smiled. "Oh good. I

wanted to see how things had changed since our last adventure here." She walked slowly out the door into the sunshine.

Standing in the same beautiful garden they had rested in on their first adventure, Mari looked around. This time, however, the benches were newly painted and no weeds could be seen anywhere. Beautiful flowers of every color peeked out from the garden and the soft grass beneath her feet was the deepest, richest green she had ever seen and spread out in every direction like a carpet. Someone was tending this garden with a master's hand.

She now remembered her last visit here as the familiar fragrances floated back to her from plants and flowers of every description. Ladybugs and butterflies flitted from bush to bush and hummingbirds were everywhere.

Sitting down to rest on one of the white benches she breathed in the aroma from a yellow flower near her that smelled like lemonade and instantly felt refreshed. Looking up she noticed Aire was not stopping and reluctantly she stood up and followed him.

Aire led them to a large white lattice archway covered in white roses. The roses climbed up the sides of the structure in front of Mari and she remembered the hedge that looked like a wall, separating the garden from the noisy busy town. But this time when the group walked through the lattice opening, Mari felt peace and the town had an air of joy.

She looked around as Aire and Nob headed to the town square to join the other Bizians. Everywhere she looked the little people were busy cooking, writing, creating music, playing instruments, telling stories and painting.

"The chaos is gone." Mari said as she felt joy welled up inside as she observed the change in the small town. "Wow, it's so peaceful, and yet, everyone's busy working."

She looked behind her and was shocked to see hundreds and hundreds of arcs. She smiled at them, glad to have their protection and help.

Aire moved into the town square and began to address the Bizians. Everyone stopped his or her work and came over to listen. The square filled up quickly.

"Fellow Bizians. You sent Nob and me on a quest to find the Hat and restore it to the land of Bizian. With the help of Mari and Mike, we journeyed into space, in a fiery chariot. After much travel, we have returned to tell you that the Hat has been found."

Mari nudged Mike. "No it hasn't!" she whispered.

Mike looked confused. "I don't get it. Why would he say that?"

Mari shook her head with a puzzled expression and then turned back to listen.

Aire raised his arms to quiet the cheers and waited until the crowd had settled down. "Prince Bob has personally informed me that the Hat will be returned here by his emissary, a person of great importance. So prepare the feast to welcome the one responsible for finding the Hat."

Mari wondered who that could possibly be.

A cheer erupted from the Bizian crowd and people began to celebrate with dances, whistles and songs. They quieted down a second time when they realized Aire had more to share.

"Bob has sent wonderful arcs from his Kingdom to live with us and help keep the peace we have recently won."

Another cheer rang out, as the arcs began to move in amongst the Bizians. Everyone shook hands with them and welcomed them with enthusiasm.

The Bizians were continually looking for a way to celebrate and eat, especially to eat. This was a perfect occasion for a feast and they began to prepare immediately.

Mari went up to Aire who was surrounded by a large group of Bizians. "I'm sorry to interrupt."

"Never feel that way, Mari. We're in your debt for restoring Bizia. How can I help you?"

"Well! You told the Bizians that the Hat would be returned, but you know, Aire, we never found it."

Aire smiled at Mari. "Prince Bob told me personally that he and a friend will be delivering the Hat to us soon."

"Oh! The friend is Philip isn't it!"

Mari clapped her hands with joy and peace flowed into her. So Philip was coming to join them.

Chapter Five

The Hat

Back on the moon, Philip felt peace flooding into him and the anxiety and despair were gone.

"Let's walk," Bob suggested.

Philip nodded. "Okay."

"My son, everything that has

happened to you up until now has a purpose and will be used in your future."

Light from Bob shone all around Philip, casting shadows on the craters and pits in the terrain all around him.

Bob continued, "Philip, I've been with you through all the difficult times of your life. It was I who lowered you down to this moon and I who influenced your grandmother to buy the house in Mike's neighborhood, so you could meet Mike and end up here."

Philip wondered if this could be true. It seemed so amazing, but looking at all that had taken place, maybe this was accurate. He listened intently to Bob's next words.

"My Father and I created a

beautiful and peaceful land. We set Governors over it to gently guide the people. A hat was created by them as a symbol of honor and love for their leader. It has been passed down from Governor to Governor, through the years."

Philip looked into Bob eyes and thought they were the kindest eyes he had ever seen. "Are you talking about Bizia and Aire?"

"Yes, Philip. Sitnaw, the evil arc, took the authority from the Bizian Governors and almost destroyed the peace of that place. With the help of Mari, Mike, and Aire, we threw out the evil and restored Bizian back to its original state of beauty and peace." Bob smiled at him.

"As a symbol of honest leadership, the people had created

a unique hat for the Governors to wear. When the evil one left, unknown to the Bizian people, he took the Hat with him. Now the people want the Hat restored to its proper owner. You can help with this, Philip."

"How?" For the very first time Philip didn't feel the need to give his opinion and he listened to Bob's reply.

"The Hat is hidden, on this obscure planetary satellite. Sitnaw knew the Bizians would not be able to find it here in space. This was done out of meanness."

"So the Hat's here on this moon?" Philip was amazed at the coincidence. He had fallen onto the very moon that Sitnaw's followers had buried the Hat.

"Philip, this was not a

coincidence. I brought you here and together we will find the Hat."

"This hat business sounds silly, but I guess I'd like to help the people of Bizia."

"That's good. Thinking of others and wanting to help them will be the beginning of healing for you, son."

Philip looked up at Bob. "Where do we look first?"

Bob began to blow on the ground and wind and dust swirled around them. A hole appeared, and then a huge cavern was uncovered, dropping down into the moon's interior.

Bob climbed over the side and lowered himself down into the dark hole.

"What are you doing?" Philip yelled.

"Follow me. Don't be afraid," echoed back.

But Philip remembered falling out of the chariot. "Don't want to fall again. I can't go in there, sorry."

"I will be with you, son. Don't forget that you are no longer alone."

The light surrounding Bob had disappeared inside the cavern and Philip didn't want to be left alone on the surface of this strange cold moon.

He peered over the side of the hole and watched Bob climbing slowly down. Light radiated off him, chasing away the darkness. He was using rocks jutting out from the walls as steps to descend into the depths.

Philip carefully climbed into the cavern and slowly lowered

himself from rock to rock like Bob.

After a long time he realized he was about halfway down the cave. Blackness filled the cavern, but the glow radiating from Bob continued to fill their area with light.

As Philip looked up to the opening above he was not watching his step and missed the next rock. For a moment he wobbled back and forth trying to regain his balance. Letting out a scream, he felt himself falling again into the darkness below. But this time there were no hands to catch him.

When he landed, he created a huge splash as a pool of water at the bottom of the cavern enclosed around his body. He came up out of the freezing water sputtering and coughing, but alive and shaken. Bob was standing on the shore watching him.

After swimming to Bob, he crawled out. "Why didn't you rescue me, like you did when I fell out of the chariot?"

"It wasn't necessary this time. You could handle this one. And you learned an important lesson."

"What?" Philip felt confused.

Bob looked at him with tenderness. "Sometimes you need to fall and not be rescued, then you find out things about yourself and others. You discover ways to avoid falling again. If I always rescue you, then you'll miss important lessons in your life."

"Well I wasn't paying attention when I fell-"

Bob finished the sentence. "-And it was a dangerous situation.

You should have been paying attention."

"Oh." Philip became quiet, taking in what had just said.

Bob motioned him to follow and they walked toward the back of the cave.

Suddenly Philip saw a colorful hat scrunched up behind some rocks and turned to Bob. "Is this it, the hat we're searching for?"

"Yes, Philip. That is the Governor's Hat. The Bizian people made it themselves."

Philip picked up the Hat and dusted it off. He thought it looked ridiculous with the blue and green vertical stripes on the sides and the bright red top. *Who'd want to wear this?* He decided to try it on. When he did, ideas filled his mind about ruling the Bizian people himself.

And he thought that, at last, he would be treated the way he deserved, with respect and honor. "I want to keep the Hat. I might be a good leader to the Bizians."

Bob looked at Philip intently. "Stolen authority never works, son. You'd end up like the evil one and his minions doing mean and hateful things to innocent people."

Philip thought about this and slowly, very slowly took the Hat off and gave it reluctantly to Bob.

"Don't be afraid. You will have a fulfilling life, my son. You won't rule the Bizian people, but you were never meant to."

"But I really want to be some-one important. I think I would be a good ruler over the Bizians."

"You have a deep hole in your heart, son. The pain from losing both your parents will not be comforted by stealing the Hat for yourself. I can give you rest from your sorrows, my son. Join me and become part of my Kingdom and help us?"

Philip was quiet and could feel tears running down his cheeks. He wiped them off with the back of his hand. "It's been really hard since mother and father died. I have not cried until now, I was too proud. But I'm beginning to understand a few things and I would like to join you, Prince Bob, and be a part of your kingdom."

"Do you believe in me, my son?"

"Yes! I do!" Philip said, changed by what Prince Bob had said and kneeling down he bowed his head. Bob rested his hand on

Philip's blond hair and said several things that I'm not going to print because they were between Philip and Prince Bob. And at that very moment the two of them vanished from the planet.

Chapter Six

The Father

When Philip looked around, he was no longer on the cold, dark moon but in a huge, warmly lit room that appeared to have no walls or ceiling. It was filled with thousands and thousands of people, animals, birds, and other unusual creatures, standing together, facing forward.

A brilliant amber light seemed to come from everywhere at once and there was a plush, expensive feeling to the room as if it had been created for royalty. Philip thought of England and his queen. She would be very comfortable here.

The amber light reflecting in the room made it hard to see and the King on the throne seemed to be the source of the brilliance.

Bob walked up the steps hand in hand with Philip to the exquisite throne.

Overwhelmed by the beauty and peace surrounding him, Philip wasn't able to analyze this moment because his scientific mind wasn't working. He was in the presence of a very great and powerful King and writing in his journal was wiped from his mind as he looked around the vast room.

Prince Bob sat down next to the King and leaned close to give him a big hug and was not the least bit intimidated or afraid of this Ruler. He turned and introduced the King to Philip.

The voice of the monarch was deep, sounding like the movement of many waters. "Welcome, my son. Come sit next to me."

Philip was in shock when he heard these words and he couldn't get his legs to respond. Thankfully Bob came over and helped him to sit next to the King. (He found out later that this King was Bob's Father.)

"You have suffered much in your young life, son. I am sorry that you lost your parents to death. But I will be a father to you. Do you wish this?"

Philip felt tears forming in his eyes. *Not now, don't cry, what a time to do such a childish thing.*

"Your tears are not childish. I understand your pain." The King put his arm around Philip and held him.

"Y-y-you can r-read my thoughts?" Philip stammered.

"Why yes, my son. I know all things. It is all right. You are safe with me."

Philip broke down and sobbed right there in the throne room. He felt such love and kindness coming from Bob's Father that all the sadness and sorrow inside burst forth like a flood. Finally a deep quiet fell over him.

He felt so safe in the Father's arms. He looked over and saw Bob watching him with such kindness in his eyes.

Bob's Father spoke again. "You can always open your heart to me, son. Bob and I care about you; you are part of our Kingdom, Philip."

Philip looked up into the kind face of the King. "Bob explained to me that he rescued our world from the evil one. I have accepted his Kingdom and all he's done."

"Good, son. Now accept me as your Father."

Philip threw his arms around the King and buried his head in the embrace. It seemed like hours, maybe days that he rested in the Father's arms. Healing flowed into his mind, body, soul and spirit and he knew that he would never feel alone again. Peace soaked into every part of him, and finally he fell into a deep sleep.

He was gently awakened by Bob placing a hand on his arm. It seemed as if days had passed.

"Time to go. We need to help your friends now."

"Oh yeah, I forgot."

Philip got up and waved good-bye to the King reluctantly. He was glad to hear these words as the King waved back:

"Do not fear my son; I am with you, always."

Those words comforted him as he took Bob's hand to leave.

Suddenly he was standing in a strange land unlike anything he had ever seen. He had arrived in the land of Bizia.

Chapter Seven

The Temptation

Philip looked around and then turned in a full circle. Roses, daffodils, ferns and large oak trees surrounded him, but where was Bob? The soft grass beneath his feet was the deepest green and spread out in every direction like a carpet.

Everywhere he looked, there were vibrant colors and wonderful fragrances floating back to him from plants and flowers of every description. Hummingbirds flitted from flower to flower and he could hear birds chirping in a nearby tree.

In his hand he held the crazy Bizian hat that he and Bob had found in the cavern on the moon. Studying it for a minute, he decided to put it on and see if anything happened. *But hadn't Bob told him to give it to the Bizian people?*

"It's not going to hurt anyone if I see how it feels. I'll only wear it for a little while." He spoke the words out loud to reassure himself about what he was doing.

As he put the hat on, he looked around him, nothing had changed. *Well, it doesn't work anyway*, he thought to himself.

Then suddenly a glowing man appeared in the distance walking slowly toward him. He was dressed in glittery clothing that shined with a strange light. The gleam reflected off him and he was beautiful to look at. Philip thought for a minute it was Bob.

"Hello there, Philip." As the man smiled, Philip thought he was very handsome. "I'm glad you tried the hat on. It's fine for you to wear it and *keep it*, if you like. Bob says some silly things."

Philip liked the sound of that. His mind filled with ideas and a story took shape: Mike and Mari were bowing down to him and calling him king Philip, and all the little Bizians were surrounding him and bowing down to him as well.

Philip was really enjoying his vision when the man interrupted, which was very irritating. Philip frowned and then lowered his eye lids in a glare.

The shining one laughed. "Come with me, Philip, there's much to do. Do you want to rule this world?"

"Yes, very much."

The man smiled, but Philip noticed it was not a nice smile. Suddenly Bob's face came into his mind and he compared his smile to the stranger's grin and felt very uncomfortable.

"Excuse me sir, but Bob told me to take this hat to the Bizians and give it to the one in authority there."

"And do you always do everything you are told?" The brazen

man laughed, but it wasn't a nice laugh which made Philip even more troubled.

He thought about Bob's Father and the deep love and safety he had felt in his arms. Alarm was slowly growing in Philip now. "Excuse me, but exactly who are you? I don't think we've been introduced." He tried to say this with confidence even though his stomach was in knots.

"I am Sitnaw. I am many things and called by many names. I rule over all that will accept my rule."

"Are you friends with Bob and his Father?"

The man laughed. "No, I'm not. They have too many silly rules and regulations. Do you want to be free, Philip? Would you like to do whatever you want without their rules? You don't have to listen to them, you can come with me and I'll make you famous. I will make you great and powerful and you can rule over the Bizian people."

Philip's stomach tightened and he felt fear gripping him like a fist. "I've already told Bob and his Father that I want to be part of their Kingdom, and I don't get the feeling you're part of it. Are you?"

"No Philip, I left their realm a long time ago. It's too late for you anyway, you put the hat on and disobeyed Bob. He and his Father won't accept you back. They're big on obeying what they say. It's too late, so why not enjoy the power you crave and join me."

While Sitnaw had been speaking, several dark figures

appeared and circled around Philip. They whispered while they made strange movements with their hands.

Suddenly he remembered the hat was still on his head. *Wonder if I take this hat off and return it, will this all end?*

Try it, floated into his mind. As he looked at the dark figures, he realized they were spinning a web of shadowy gloom all around him. In a few minutes he would be in a cocoon of the black netting.

Looking up at the shiny man, Philip saw that he was laughing again and it was a most alarming laugh. Panic welled up inside him and his heart beat so hard, he thought it would jump out of his chest. Making a decision, he pulled the hat off his head.

This time there was silence, the glowing man and the dark figures were gone. He was standing by himself in the beautiful garden, filled with flowers of every color and he could hear birds chirping and see butterflies flitting from bush to bush.

There was a stir next to him and when he looked over, Bob was standing there.

"I-I am s-sorry." Philip stuttered awkwardly.

"I am very glad you took the Hat off, Philip. Stolen authority will only make you a puppet for evil."

"Do y-you f-forgive me?" Philip stammered.

Bob looked at him with such kindness in his eyes and smiled. This was a genuine smile, full of love and life. Philip compared it to

Sitnaw's smile and shivered.

"Of course I forgive you, Philip. You've learned an important lesson today. I explained the Hat to you, when we were on the moon. I had hoped the information would protect you from the evil one."

"Is it too late for me to be in your Kingdom? Sitnaw said it was because I disobeyed."

Bob looked deep into Philip's eyes. "He's an evil arc that wars with our Kingdom. It's never too late if you apologize and then change what you are doing."

Philip hung his head and pulled at a blade of grass.

Bob reached out and put his hand on Philip's shoulder. "Now will you do what I asked and deliver the Hat to the Bizian people? They've been waiting a long time and the enemy almost stole it from them again."

Philip looked up at Bob and then offered him the Hat. Then he slipped his hand in Bob's. "I'm ready now. Can we go?"

"Yes. Well done, you made the right choice."

Together they walked through the lovely garden and into a square, where a large group of Bizians were gathered

Chapter Eight

The Reunion

When the Bizians saw Bob, they ran toward him, laughing. Surrounding him, they peppered him with questions.

Philip felt overwhelmed with the large crowd and gradually moved toward the outside of the circle.

He turned around to study the new land. What he saw was a lovely park-like area that had white lattice arches with roses and vines growing up the sides. Benches and tables were scattered around with little pits made for cooking.

Everywhere he looked Bizians were busy making preparations for a great feast. Gardeners were creating beautiful flower arrangements and setting them down on long tables. He could hear wisps of music floating through the air as singers practiced their songs. When he looked in the direction of the melody he saw musicians writing down the music with colorful ink on elegant scrolls.

The aroma of cooking drew Philip over to watch bakers rolling out dough and chopping up fruit.

There were plates piled high with meats, vegetables and sweet desserts and also jugs filled with drink of every kind. He suddenly realized he had not eaten in a very long time.

One of the cooks waved him over and told him to pick some food from the plates in front of him. When he had chosen, the cook handed him a mug filled with a cold sweet juice.

But the thing that captivated Philip the most was the artists' use of oils and colorful paints to create beauty on canvas. He stood in awe, watching the stunning scenery come to life.

At that moment Bob came walking up with Mari and Mike. When Mari saw Philip she ran and hugged him with tears in her eyes.

"Oh, Philip, I thought you'd died. You fell out of the chariot, it - it was frightening. Don't know how you survived such a fall."

Philip looked up. "I was protected by Bob. He stayed with me and helped me find the Hat. Mike and Mari, I went to his Kingdom and met his Father and now he is my Father too."

He saw Mari's eyes light up when he mentioned Bob's Father.

She looked at him and smiled. "We had an opportunity to be with Bob's Father too. It was amazing and I'll never forget it. You got to meet him also. How wonderful."

Bob put his hand on Philip's shoulder. "We must go now and join the Bizians. Time to return their Hat."

"Can I come back and watch

the artists paint?"

Bob laughed. "Why yes, Philip. So you enjoy watching them create those beautiful works of art?"

"Very much."

"Well, when you come back, I'll set you up with paints and an easel of your own."

"Would you? Can't think of anything I'd rather try." Philip had a hard time tearing his eyes away from the beautiful paintings.

Bob smiled at him. "You may have found a hidden talent, my young friend."

Bob took off toward a group of Bizians in the center of town. Philip followed with Mari and Mike at his side.

"That's the one," said Aire as he pointed to Philip.

"Yes, he's the one," Nob chimed in.

Philip realized with shock that they were referring to him. *Oh no, they found out what I did*. He hung his head in shame and looked at the ground and sighed.

All of a sudden a loud roar surrounded him and he realized it was clapping. The Bizian people were applauding him, cheering and shouting his name.

Bob turned to him. "Come with me. Time to give the Hat to the Bizian people."

As he walked with Bob through the center of the crowd he heard people whispering his name as he passed. Mike and Mari were right beside him and he felt safe, surrounded by his friends.

They headed to a platform in

the middle of town. It had steps going up to a simple stage that had been raised a few feet above the ground.

Bob and Philip stood on one side while Aire and Nob stood on the other, facing the Bizian people. The crowd quieted down as everyone waited for Bob to speak.

"Beloved Bizians. You've waited patiently for this day. Now it has finally arrived. Philip is the one who retrieved the stolen Hat from a far moon and almost died trying." He turned to Philip. "Now is the time, son, to give the Hat back to the Bizian people. Aire, step forward please."

Philip now realized what he must do and as Aire stepped forward he bowed and handed him the Hat. Loud applause rang out from the crowd and many Bizians shouted and whistled.

Bob stood next to him and spoke softly. "You have made the right choice, son, and I'm proud of you. Always knew you would." Bob smiled warmly and put his arm around him.

At that moment, Philip felt peace flooding him and understood the important lesson he had just learned. Realizing Aire was now speaking, he focused back on what was being said.

"Thank you, Philip, and Prince Bob, for finding and returning this treasured Bizian Hat." Applause erupted and Aire held his hands up for silence again.

"People of Bizian, I've loved serving you as your Governor, but after having a long talk with Prince

Bob, I understand that another is ready to govern. The time has come for me to step down and be an advisor. You all know how I love my solitude." Aire looked at the silent and confused crowd. "Nob, will you step forward please."

Every eye was on Nob, who wasn't aware that he had been addressed but stood quietly looking at Aire. Suddenly his face turned red as he realized all eyes were on him. Slowly, he walked over to Aire, with a puzzled expression on his face.

"And now," Prince Bob smiled at Aire approvingly and turned to the young Bizian. "Nob, it is with great expectation that I present you with this Hat and authorize you to govern my beloved people of Bizia. I entrust them into your care. Be kind and gentle, always ready to serve them."

Nob bowed low to Prince Bob and accepted the Hat. "Thank you" was all he could get out, which the Bizians seemed to approve for they responded with applause, shouting and cheering all at once.

They especially liked that he was not long winded or one to give lengthy boring speeches. His short thank you, at this occasion, won him the reputation of being the Governor of few words and he became a much beloved and kind ruler to the people of Bizian.

Philip walked down the steps to where Mike and Mari were watching in the front row.

"Wow! Was that surprising." His face turned red.

"You were great, Philip." Mari

smiled at him and Mike nodded.

He thought about the Hat and the memory of Mari and Mike and the Bizian people bowing to him.

He began to understand what Prince Bob was trying to show him. Maybe giving away authority to the rightful person was better than keeping it yourself. He felt good about his choice today.

Then the celebration began. The Bizian people are known for their wonderful parties. Philip eyed a long wooden table laden with every kind of food and drink, and joined the line to fill his plate high with every delicacy.

Looking for the others, he finally spotted Mari and headed in her direction. As he moved toward her, several Bizians smiled at him and reached out a hand to shake the one who had found their treasured Hat.

Mari sat at a table with Bob, Mike, Aire and Nob, and Philip plopped down next to them.

"Congratulations, Nob, on becoming the next boss over Bizia." Philip took Nob's hand to shake it.

"Thank you, Philip. But we see the Governorship as a way to serve the people of Bizian rather than boss them around. But I understand your sentiments."

That was enough talk for both Nob and Philip. They each got to work on the wonderful plate of food in front of them.

After the meal, musicians brought out instruments Philip had never seen before, and played with skill while groups of Bizians sang along in harmony. He wanted to listen to the songs all night long, but Bob said it was time to go.

"I don't want to leave."

Bob smiled at him and reached out his hand.

Philip got up and followed Bob to say good-bye to Aire and Nob.

Bob gave both Aire and Nob a big hug and everyone said their good-byes. "You have governed my people well, Aire. And now it's good that you are releasing your caring leadership to one who will rule them as you have."

Philip felt wetness fall onto his cheeks and realized his eyes were filling up with tears. He was surprised by the emotion he felt for those he had just met.

He turned and followed Bob in the direction of the old tree.

Chapter Nine

The Return Journey

Bob moved through the town and into the beautiful garden near the old tree entrance. He stopped and turned toward the children. "Thank you for all your help in returning the Hat to its rightful owners. Philip, you had a difficult choice but in the end you made the right decision. I'm proud of you. Now, are you three ready to go home?"

Mari yawned. "I don't even know what time it is back home. This adventure started in the middle of the night."

"Well, not exactly the middle of the night. Eleven thirty, I think, was the actual time," Mike said playfully.

"Oh, stop it; I'm too tired for this. Where's the old tree?" She turned toward Bob.

Philip could feel his energy disappearing as well. "Yeah, where is that tree?"

Bob laughed. "Follow me."

For what seemed like half an hour, Philip followed Bob through the land of Bizia. Finally he sat down on one of the benches. "Where's that tree. Going to rest for a moment."

Mari sat down next to him. "Me too!"

Bob pointed. "Look, Philip, it's right in front of you."

There was the old tree with a gap big enough to crawl through. *At last, now I can go home and rest.* Philip stood up.

Bob walked right through the trunk of the tree while Mike dropped onto all fours and crawled through the opening with Mari behind him. Philip followed her, breathing loudly.

"Hang in there, Philip, just a little farther." She stood up in the familiar interior of the tree.

Standing up next to her, he smiled weakly.

Bob patted him on the back. "You've done well. I'm proud of you and so is my Father."

Philip liked hearing that. He no longer felt tired. In fact a new spurt of energy surged through his body. He stood up straight, putting his shoulders back and looked at Bob.

Bob looked back at him and laughed "Ready to go home?"

"Yes," everyone said in unison.

"You will each be returned to your bedroom at the exact time this adventure started."

"What? That's impossible!" Philip looked at Bob in disbelief.

"All things are possible with me. Have faith."

As Bob was speaking Philip noticed his voice sounded farther and farther away. The interior of the old tree faded while his bedroom became more and more visible. He walked over to his bed and crawled in, laying his head on the soft pillow. Pulling the warm comforter over his shoulders, he turned over and fell into a deep sleep, unaware that he had left his favorite journal in the land of Bizia.

Look for the other books in this series on Amazon.com under Tricia Martin, *The Old Tree Series,* in the children's books.

The Old Tree; A Wonderful Edu-taining Adventure by Laurel A Basbas Ph.D. Author

"Tricia Martin's enlightening little book, "The Old Tree" is a delightful, spirited adventure with enchanting, lovable characters and a spiritually uplifting message. It is edu-tainment (education and entertainment) to be enjoyed by youngsters and by those wise enough to be young at heart. It is an invitation to color outside the lines, to see into the invisible, and to grow much larger and much smaller (as Alice in Wonderland would tell you) all in the same story. Tricia's tale entreats you to enjoy the realm of the impossibly possible! I for one, enjoyed the ride."

Sheneau Stanley

"Tricia, uses stories to share valuable life lessons and underlying important values that kids must have to have successful lives today."

Desi d'Amani

"Enter the world of imagination, intrigue, and adventure! Whether young or younger still the Old Tree is a door into a mystical adventure where life isn't always as it appears to be and lessons are learned through overcoming. This book invites children to explore how decisions affect the world around and beyond them and it allows the childlike to re-embrace the realities of the once real but forgotten invisible realm. Step through the door into an adventure that will cause you to rethink the world as you once perceived it.

The Old Tree Series may very well be like a Chronicles of Narnia for this generation."

R. Gutierrez

The Old Tree is a portal into a kingdom where courage, hope and the promise of a new day reminds one of love's enduring presence."

Christy Peters

"Love this book. The story takes the reader on an incredible adventure. I love how Tricia was able to incorporate things from the extra-terrestrial (spirit realm) and show how they can be just as real and merged into the lives of those of us who live on the terrestrial plain. Well done and an enjoyable read for child or adult!"

Now available in paperback and e-book

The first book in The Old Tree Series

The Old Tree

Tricia Martin

Mike is bored with his summer routine. He meets a new neighbor, Mari, and together they step through an unusual tree and journey to another realm with a loving and powerful new friend. When they return home, they find a battle raging and their young lives are changed forever.

Now available in paperback and e-book

The second book in The Old Tree Series

The Land Of Bizia

Tricia Martin

Mike and Mari find themselves in
a world that is on the verge of
destroying itself through
busyness. With the help of their
loving and powerful friend, Bob,
they hope to bring the people of
Bizia back to the values and peace
they once knew.

Now available in paperback and e-book

The third book in The Old Tree Series

The Kingdom Of Knon

Tricia Martin

Bob takes Mike and Mari to an underwater kingdom in search of an important book that has been stolen.

Now available in paperback and e-book

The fourth book in The Old Tree Series

The Mild, Mild West

Tricia Martin

Mike and Mari join an unusual creature from Bob's realm and find themselves in a western world. They need to find a way to rescue young people being stolen from their families.

Now available in paperback and e-book

The sixth book in The Old Tree Series

Arabian Lights

Tricia Martin

Mari's father and sister, as children, discover an unusual tree. When they walk through it they find themselves in an arid desert where a great adventure awaits them.

Now available in paperback and e-book

The seventh book in The Old Tree Series

One For All and All for One

Tricia Martin

Everything created is on the verge of destruction. Bob asks Mike and Mari to help him solve this problem.

I wanted to put a British boy in this adventure because I have fond memories of living in England when I was a young girl.

Made in the USA
Charleston, SC
03 March 2015